CN00956756

Merry Christmas, WOODY

By Kristen L. Depken

A Random House PICTUREBACK® Book

Random House 🏠 New York

Copyright © 2013 Disney/Pixar. All rights reserved. Slinky® Dog is a registered trademark of Poof-Slinky, Inc.
© Poof-Slinky, Inc. Playskool Rockin' Robot Mr. Mike® is a registered trademark of Hasbro, Inc. Used with permission.
© Hasbro, Inc. Etch A Sketch® © The Ohio Art Company. All rights reserved. Published in the United States by
Random House Children's Books, a division of Random House, Inc., 1745 Broadway, New York, NY 10019, and
in Canada by Random House of Canada Limited, Toronto, in conjunction with Disney Enterprises, Inc. Pictureback,
Random House, and the Random House colophon are registered trademarks of Random House, Inc.
randomhouse.com/kids
ISBN 978-0-7364-3070-8
Printed in the United States of America
10 9 8 7

It was almost Christmas! Buzz Lightyear, Rex, and all the other toys were excited—except for Sheriff Woody.

Woody wanted to find presents for his friends. But he didn't know what to get them!

Buzz Lightyear was planning a big Christmas party.

"It's going to be the best toy Christmas ever!" he told Woody.

"I can't wait," said Woody halfheartedly. He only had two days to find the perfect presents.

"Wheezy, do you want anything special for Christmas this year?" Woody asked.

"Just for my voice not to crack during my big performance," replied the penguin. He was going to sing at Buzz's Christmas party. "I have to get back to my rehearsal now, okay?"

Woody sighed. Wheezy had not been any help!

Woody found Jessie on the mantel, decorating for the party.

"Jessie, what do you want for Christmas this year?" asked Woody.

"Just the best party ever!" replied Jessie. "I hope I can finish decorating in time."

Woody still didn't know what gifts to give!

Soon it was Christmas Eve. Buzz gave each toy a job to help get ready for the party.

"Oh, I can't wait!" exclaimed Rex.

Buzz, Jessie, and Bo Peep wrapped presents.

The Aliens and the Green Army Men made a tree out of cotton balls.

Hamm and Rex piled the presents under the tree.

"A little to the left," said Hamm. "Nope. Now a little to the right."

Everyone worked hard!

Buzz and Jessie dressed Rex up like Santa Claus.
"Just call me Santa Rex," said Rex. "Ho, ho, *roar!*"
The Green Army Men turned RC into Santa's sled.
It was almost time for the party!

"Wow, that looks great, guys!" said Woody when he saw the Christmas tree.

But he was worried. He still hadn't found the perfect presents for his friends.

"Buzz, what should I do? I haven't gotten presents for anyone yet!" said Woody as the party was starting. "I don't know if I can come to the party." "Don't be silly, cowboy," said Buzz. "Come on."

Buzz led Woody to where Bo Peep was reading the toys a Christmas story.
"Does it look like anyone is worried about presents?" asked Buzz.
"Well, no . . . ," said Woody.

Just then, Buzz called all the toys around the tree.
"Get the lights!" he said.

Sarge turned the lights out, and Buzz used his laser
to create a Christmas light show.

"Wow!" cried Woody. It was magical!

It suddenly didn't matter whether Woody had
presents—all that mattered was spending Christmas
with his friends.

"Guys! Look!" cried Woody when the light show was over. "Snow!"
He led everyone to the window, where they watched the snow fall softly outside.
"Now, *that's* what I'd call a perfect present," said Buzz.

© Disney/Pixar

© Disney/Pixar

© Disney/Pixar

© Disney/Pixar